Honestly, OUR MUSIC STOLE THE SHOW!

The Story of
THE BREMEN TOWN MUSICIANS
as Told by THE
DONKEY

by **Jessica Gunderson**

illustrated by **Cristian Bernardini**

PICTURE WINDOW BOOKS
a capstone imprint

Editor: Jill Kalz
Designer: Lori Bye
Premedia Specialist: Tori Abraham
The illustrations in this book were created digitally.

 o⚬ᵔ❧✤ᶜᵒ⚬o

Picture Window Books
1710 Roe Crest Drive
North Mankato, MN 56003
www.mycapstone.com

Library of Congress Cataloging-in-Publication data
is available on the Library of Congress website.
ISBN 978-1-5158-2296-7 (library binding)
ISBN 978-1-5158-2316-2 (paperback)
ISBN 978-1-5158-2300-1 (eBook PDF)
Summary: The Bremen Town Musicians never wanted to be heroes.
They wanted a recording contract! At least that's the story readers hear from
the donkey's point of view in this charming twist on the classic fairy tale
"The Bremen Town Musicians."

Printed and bound in the United States of America.
010847S18

Welcome to the Bremen Town Theater! I'm Don Key, leader of the musical group Don Key and the Lucky Three. For our shows, I *don* a bowtie and sing on *key*. Get it? DON KEY? Also, I'm a *donkey*. Ha!

But I wasn't always a famous singer. It happened by accident. Get comfy, and I'll tell you *my* side of the story.

Since I was little, I wanted to be a singer.

The other animals laughed at me. "You'll never be a musician," they said. "You're a donkey. Donkeys haul hay and pull wagons."

But I didn't let them crush my dreams. No! Every night I practiced. I sang loud and proud. **"Hee-HAAAAAW! Hee-HAAAAAW!"**

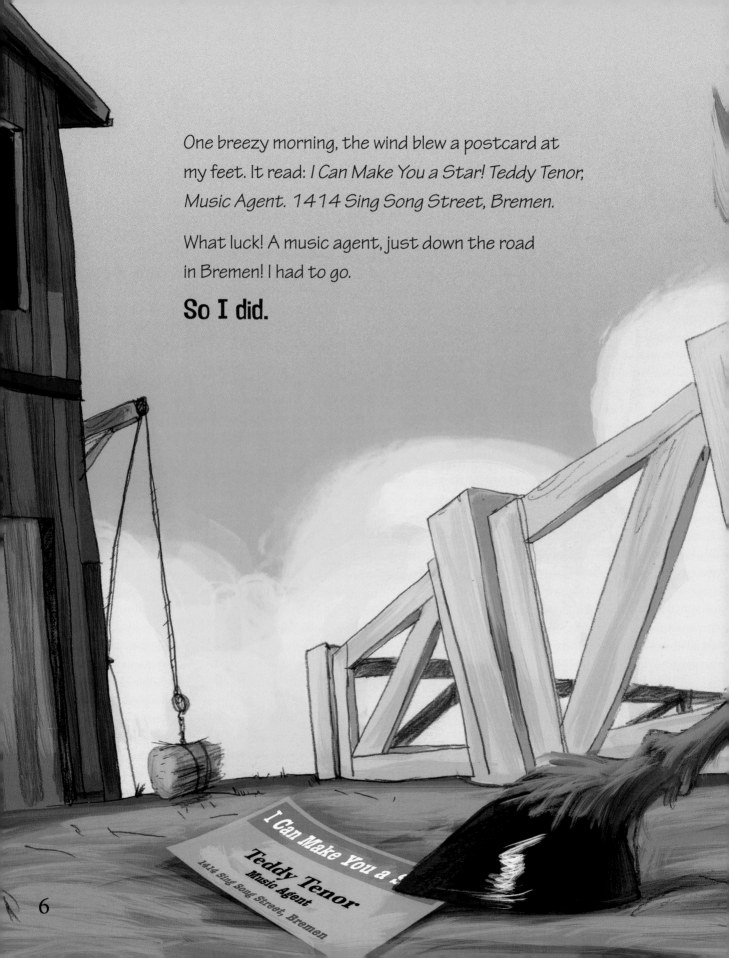

One breezy morning, the wind blew a postcard at my feet. It read: *I Can Make You a Star! Teddy Tenor, Music Agent. 1414 Sing Song Street, Bremen.*

What luck! A music agent, just down the road in Bremen! I had to go.

So I did.

I Can Make You a S
Teddy Tenor
Music Agent
1414 Sing Song Street, Bremen

Later that day, as I was trotting along, singing my songs, I tripped over a log. But it wasn't a log. It was a dog.

"AAA-OOOH!" the dog howled.

"Bravo!" I said. "How long have you been an opera singer?"

"Opera?" the dog said. "I howled because you stepped on my tail."

"Sorry. Well, you have a lovely voice," I said. "I'm going to Bremen to get a record deal. Join me!"

"Thank you," she said. "Sounds fun. My name's Lucy Dog-a-rotti."

After a little while, Lucy and I came upon a cat, napping in a hat.

"MEE-OWWWZA! Howdy, y'all," she sang.

"Such an amazing voice you have!" I told her. "We're going to Bremen to get a record deal. Join us!"

"Thank you," she said. "Name's Catsy Kline."

Soon Lucy, Catsy, and I heard a loud sound above our heads.
We looked up and saw a rooster perched on a streetlight.

"ROCK-A-DOO! ROCK-A-DOODLE-DOO!" he crowed.

"I'm Punky Rooster, and I want to be a rock star!"

"Hello!" I said. "We're going to Bremen to get a record deal. Join us!"

The rooster nodded, and our group was complete.

As night fell, we came to Sing Song Street.

"What's the address?" Lucy asked.

I thought hard. "Um . . . 4411? 1144? 4141?"

"4141 is the cottage right here," Punky said.

I knocked on the door. No answer. I peeked through the window. "I see *three* agents in there!" I whispered. "What luck!"

"Let's just start singing and surprise them," Lucy suggested.

"Excellent idea!" I said.

"On the count of three," I said. "One . . . two . . . three!"

Hee-HAAAAAAW! Hee-HAAAAAAW! AAA-OOOH! MEE-OWWWZA! ROCK-A-DOO! ROCK-A-DOODLE-DOO!

The agents' eyes popped open.

"What *is* that?" the first man yelled.

"I don't know!" the second man shouted.

"It's terrifying!" the third man hollered. "Let's get out of here!"

And with that, the agents scrambled out the door and ran into the forest.

"What happened?" Catsy moaned. "I thought we sounded good."

"You were off-key," Lucy said.

"No, *you* were singing the wrong words," Punky snapped.

"I guess we just have to keep practicing," I said.

Catsy nodded toward the food on the table inside the cottage. "Maybe a snack first?" she asked.

So we ate a little . . . OK, a LOT . . . and then fell asleep on the floor.

Well, the agents came back! But we didn't know they were there. And *they* didn't know *we* were there.

I woke to yelling, scratching, barking, kicking . . . and the agents running out the door.

"What happened?" I cried. "What made them run away *this* time?"

I just opened my eyes and saw a man looking at me. I didn't *mean* to scratch him!

I thought Catsy was being attacked, so I bit the man's leg. I didn't know it was one of the agents!

I buried my face in my hooves. "We'll *never* get a record deal," I said.

"Wait. Listen," Lucy said.

I stopped sobbing. "It sounds like clapping," I said.

Catsy opened the door. There, in the yard, was the biggest crowd of people I'd ever seen. When they saw us, they cheered.

"They must want us to sing," Catsy whispered.

"Then let's sing!" I said. "One . . . two . . . *three*!"

Truthfully, we gave the best concert of our lives.

Before our final song, a well-dressed man handed me a card — a card I'd seen before.

"Teddy Tenor, music agent," he said. "You guys are fantastic! I'd love to give you a record deal."

"Great!" I said. "But . . . if *you're* Teddy Tenor, then who were those —?"

"Mr. Key," a reporter called out, "tell me, how does it feel to be a hero? Bremen is very lucky you and your band scared away the area's most dangerous gang of robbers."

"Robbers?" I said. "I . . . uh . . ."

21

"ROCK-A-DOODLE-DOO!" crowed Punky.

"Yeah," I told the reporter, "like Punky said. It feels **hee-HAAAAAWESOME!"**

And that, my friends, is how we came to be Don Key and the Lucky Three.

Pretty cool, huh?

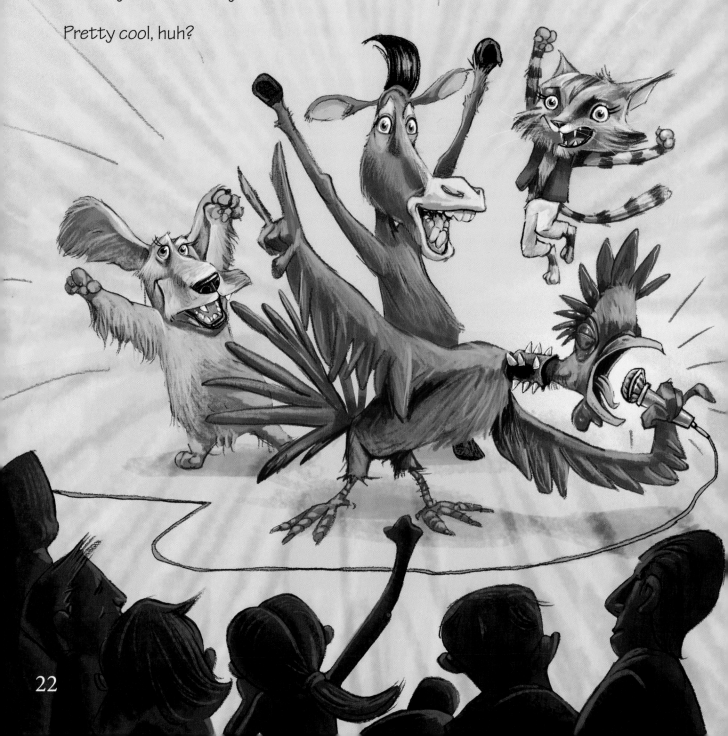

Think About It

Describe each of the Bremen Town Musicians. Use the illustrations to help you describe how the animals look and act.

A number of characters mention "luck" in the story. Why do you think Don Key says, "What luck!" near the beginning of the story? Why does the reporter say the town is lucky? How are Don Key and his band lucky?

This version of the story is told from the donkey's point of view. How might the story change if it were told from the robbers' point of view?

Look online to find the original story. Compare it to this version. How are the two versions alike? How are they different?

Glossary

character—a person, animal, or creature in a story
point of view—a way of looking at something
version—an account of something from a certain point of view

Read More

Blair, Eric. *The Bremen Town Musicians: A Retelling of the Grimms' Fairy Tale.* My First Classic Story. Mankato, Minn.: Picture Window Books, 2011.

Wildsmith, Brian, retold and illustrated by. *The Bremen Town Musicians.* New York: Star Bright Books, 2012.

Internet Sites

Use FactHound to find Internet sites related to this book.

Visit *www.facthound.com*

Just type in 9781515822967 and go.

Look for all the books in the series:

Believe Me, Goldilocks Rocks!

Believe Me, I Never Felt a Pea!

For Real, I Paraded in My Underpants!

Frankly, I'd Rather Spin Myself a New Name!

Frankly, I Never Wanted to Kiss Anybody!

Honestly, Our Music Stole the Show!

Honestly, Red Riding Hood Was Rotten!

Listen, My Bridge Is SO Cool!

No Kidding, Mermaids Are a Joke!

No Lie, I Acted Like a Beast!

No Lie, Pigs (and Their Houses) CAN Fly!

Really, Rapunzel Needed a Haircut!

Seriously, Cinderella Is SO Annoying!

Seriously, Snow White Was SO Forgetful!

Truly, We Both Loved Beauty Dearly!

Trust Me, Hansel and Gretel Are SWEET!

Trust Me, Jack's Beanstalk Stinks!

Truthfully, Something Smelled Fishy!

Super-cool stuff! Check out projects, games and lots more at
www.capstonekids.com